Always follow your dreams!

- Mit Bg

Reading:
the key to unlocking imagination.

Dedicated to Mckinley

MICKALO ELEPHO

Loves Adventures So

Written and Illustrated By
Martine Barjon

Chocolate milk, she loves to sip
until it's all gone,
every last drip!

But she is a queen
and can always have more.

Daddy won't say no
this is for sure.

Bathtime for Mickalo
is time to play.
She can splash in the tub
all throughout the day.

Sometimes Mickalo Elepho
makes a wish

that she can swim in the ocean,
just like a fish.

"Mickalo, my Mickalo,
you're such a good helper!"

"No problem mommy,
picking veggies is my pleasure."

She dreams of sunshine
and sunflowers.
as she plays in a field
for hours and hours.

She imagines frolicking
with a butterfly,
who also loves the flowers
that are nearby.

Her red balloon
  flies with no care.
    She rides her bike
      as it dances in the air.

When she is in the sky

she looks down
and waves at everybody in town.

She creates a city
using her colorful blocks.
Mickalo's building skills
really rock!

She says "One day you will see,
towers and houses designed by me".

Mickalo Elepho likes
to dance and sing.

It is one of her favorite things.

Dreaming she is in front of a crowd,
dancing hard and singing loud.

But what makes her most happy...

is all the love she gets
from mommy and daddy

That, she doesn't have to pretend
because their love for her
has no end!

Thank You!

Made in the USA
Lexington, KY
27 September 2017